Dear Parent:
Your child's love of reading starts here!

W9-BQS-573

Every child learns to read in a different way and at his or her own speed. Some go back and forth between reading levels and read favorite books again and again. Others read through each level in order. You can help your young reader improve and become more confident by encouraging his or her own interests and abilities. From books your child reads with you to the first books he or she reads alone, there are I Can Read Books for every stage of reading:

SHARED READING
Basic language, word repetition, and whimsical illustrations, ideal for sharing with your emergent reader

BEGINNING READING
Short sentences, familiar words, and simple concepts for children eager to read on their own

READING WITH HELP
Engaging stories, longer sentences, and language play for developing readers

READING ALONE
Complex plots, challenging vocabulary, and high-interest topics for the independent reader

ADVANCED READING
Short paragraphs, chapters, and exciting themes for the perfect bridge to chapter books

I Can Read Books have introduced children to the joy of reading since 1957. Featuring award-winning authors and illustrators and a fabulous cast of beloved characters, I Can Read Books set the standard for beginning readers.

A lifetime of discovery begins with the magical words "I Can Read!"

Visit www.icanread.com for information on enriching your child's reading experience.

I Can Read Book® is a trademark of HarperCollins Publishers.

Beat Bugs: Meet the Beat Bugs
Copyright © 2017 11:11 Creations Pty. Ltd., BEAT BUGS™, its logos, names and related indicia are trademarks of and copyrighted by 11:11 Creations Pty. Ltd. All rights reserved.
Manufactured in China.
No part of this book may be used or reproduced in any manner whatsoever without written permission except in the case of brief quotations embodied in critical articles and reviews. For information address HarperCollins Children's Books, a division of HarperCollins Publishers, 195 Broadway, New York, NY 10007.
www.icanread.com

Library of Congress Control Number: 2016949895
ISBN 978-0-06-264066-6

Typography by Brenda E. Angelilli
17 18 19 20 21 SCP 10 9 8 7 6 5 4 3 2 1   ❖   First Edition

I Can Read!

BEGINNING
1
READING

beat bugs™

Meet the Beat Bugs

adapted by Anne Lamb
Beat Bugs created by
Josh Wakely

HARPER
An Imprint of HarperCollins Publishers

Welcome to Beat Bugs Village!

Let's meet the Beat Bugs.

First up is Jay.

Jay is a beetle.

He lives in an old boot.

He loves skateboarding
and making music on his keyboard.

When he gets an ouch-ee,
he always bounces back.

Next door is Kumi!

Kumi is a ladybug.

She lives in a takeout container.

She loves karate

and exploring the backyard.

If you have any problems,

she's the best at solving them!

Buzz is the tiniest Beat Bug.

She is a fruit fly.

She lives in an old juice carton.

When Buzz gets excited,

the spinner on her hat

moves super fast!

Walter is the biggest Beat Bug.

He is a slug.

He lives in a deflated basketball.

Inside, it looks like a stage.

He loves to tell stories

and is good at singing and dancing.

Crick is a cricket.

He lives in an old paint tin.

He loves to invent new gadgets.

Crick always has the best ideas
and writes them in his notepad.

Postman Bee is a bumblebee.

He delivers the mail to everyone.

He is always there

to help the Beat Bugs.

Granny Bee is a bumblebee, too.

She is Postman Bee's grandma.

She is famous for her honey pies.

She makes some for the Beat Bugs!

Katter is a caterpillar.

She hangs out with the Beat Bugs.

She is close with Kumi.

They both love leaf cakes!

Doris is a spider.

She creates art with her webs.

She makes sure the Beat Bugs
do not get into too much trouble.

Milli is a millipede.

She has so many legs!

She is friends with the Beat Bugs.

Boris is a bullfrog.

He always has a blast in the rain.

He likes to play with the Beat Bugs.

Doctor Robert is a praying mantis.

He is also a doctor.

When the bugs are sick,

they visit Doctor Robert.

Morg is a stick insect.

He is very tall!

The Beat Bugs like him.

Alex is a stinkbug.

He can make gas,

as long as he eats golden leaves.

He helps out the Beat Bugs.

Warren is an earthworm.

The Beat Bugs call him Nowhere Man.

He cannot see that well.

But he can still find his way.

Sergeant Pepper is a beetle.

He is a ringmaster for a circus.

When his circus visits the village,
he befriends Walter.

Lucy is a dragonfly.

Her wings look like diamonds.

She has big, pretty eyes.

The Beat Bugs go far to find her.

Geoff is a cockroach.

He lives near the trash.

He cannot always be trusted.

Army Ants are ants.

They work as a team.

They help the Beat Bugs

build things.

Glowies are fuzzy glowworms.
They can glow in the dark
and are useful at night.

Octopus sits in the middle of the garden.

He is a sprinkler.

He has many arms.

He can see almost everything!

The Beat Bugs always look out

for one another,

and that's what it means

to be the best-est of friends.

Come back to Beat Bugs Village soon!